D0069167

A Pee Wee Christmas

A Pee Wee Christmas

JUDY DELTON

Illustrated by Alan Tiegreen

A YOUNG YEARLING BOOK

For Margi Mark, who is
Mrs. Peters's Baby's Grandma

Published by
Dell Publishing
a division of
The Bantam Doubleday Dell Publishing Group, Inc.
666 Fifth Avenue
New York, New York 10103

ISBN: 0-440-40067-8

Printed in the United States of America

December 1988

10 9 8 7 6 5 4 3

W

Contents

CHAPTER 1

Kindness Coupons

"Today is our last Scout meeting," said Mrs. Peters, "before Christmas. We have a lot to do today."

Mrs. Peters looks fat, thought Molly Duff. Fatter than last time the Pee Wees met. The Scouts knew their troop leader was going to have a baby soon. They couldn't wait! They might get to hold the baby and rock it. Take it for a walk. Even feed it, thought Molly.

The Scouts were in Mrs. Peters's basement. There were holiday decorations on the wall. Decorations the Pee Wees had made. Christmas trees. Stars. Menorahs.

"First," said Mrs. Peters, "let's talk about good deeds you have done this week. Have you got anything to report?"

Tracy Barnes waved her hand. "I took care of my baby sister," she said, "when my mom had to go to exercise class."

Tracy sniffled and wiped her nose on the back of her hand. Tracy had allergies. Her eyes watered and her nose ran.

Tracy had lots of brothers and sisters. "My little sister almost rolled off the bed," said Tracy. "And I caught her just in time."

Molly wondered if that was a real good deed. Not letting a baby roll off a bed.

"I bet I saved her life!" Tracy added.

"Wonderful!" said Mrs. Peters. "That was certainly a good deed! Saving a baby's life. Any others?" she asked.

Roger White was waving his hand. "I saved somebody's life. This little boy was playing near the street. A car was coming. I grabbed him and took him home."

"Well, that was wonderful, Roger," said Mrs. Peters. "It is good to look out for children who are in danger."

"You just said that because I did," whispered Tracy to Roger. "You didn't really save somebody's life."

"I did too!" shouted Roger. "I did too. Ask my mother."

"I don't believe you," said Tracy.

"Anyone else?" said Mrs. Peters.

Mary Beth Kelly raised her hand.

"Molly and I took some clothes to Goodwill for my mom," she said. "Two big bags. We walked there."

Molly nodded. She had forgotten about that good deed.

"Why, that is fine," said Mrs. Peters. "It is always good to be a help at home."

Sonny Betz was waving his hand.

"I made my bed this morning," he said.

"That's not a good deed, dummy. I make my bed every morning," said Kevin Moe.

"It is too," said Sonny. "Then my mom doesn't have to do it before she goes to work. Isn't it a good deed, Mrs. Peters?"

"We all should make our beds in the morning," said Mrs. Peters. She did not say whether it was a good deed or not.

"And I poured my own milk too," said Sonny.

"Today," said Mrs. Peters, going on to something new, "we are going to make gifts for our parents for the holidays."

The Pee Wees cheered. "Yeah!" Making presents was fun.

"Maybe we'll make cookies," whispered Lisa Ronning to Molly. "Or paperweights."

Mrs. Peters had colored paper in her hand.

Red and green and blue.

Yellow and orange and pink.

Bright colors.

Every color of the rainbow.

Colored paper is not for paperweights, thought Molly.

"I thought of a wonderful present," said Mrs. Peters. "I thought of Pee Wee Scout Kindness Coupons. A Kindness Coupon is a coupon for a favor. You give them to your parents, and they give them back to you when they need a favor."

Mrs. Peters held up the bright paper. "We will cut out different color squares. On each square you will write what the coupon is good for. Like 'one dishwashing.' Then you sign your name. When

your mother or father wants you to wash the dishes, they give you the coupon and you do the favor."

"My mom has a dishwasher," said Rachel Meyers. "We don't wash dishes by hand at my house."

Molly looked at Rachel and sighed.

But Mrs. Peters just said, "Well then, you can say you will load and unload the dishwasher, Rachel."

"Okay," said Rachel.

"On another you can write 'to Dad for one car wash.' "

Rachel's hand was waving again.

Mrs. Peters said, "If your dad has his car washed at the car wash, you can say you will sweep out the garage instead."

Rachel's hand went down.

"Do you get the idea?" said Mrs. Peters. "You can make as many coupons as you like, and you can choose any

8

favor you wish," she said. "Just be sure you don't write more than you can do."

Everyone was thinking of ideas for coupons.

"My mom loves it when I polish the silver," said Patty Baker. "I can make a coupon for that."

"Great!" said Mrs. Peters. "That's the idea. Think about what would be a nice holiday favor at your house. Then I will write it on this blackboard so you will spell it right."

"I can spell dishwasher myself," said Rachel.

"I can spell anything," said Kevin. "I get an A in spelling every time."

"Well, just in case," said Mrs. Peters.

Mrs. Peters passed out the colored paper. Then she passed out envelopes to put the coupons in. And a Christmas seal of Santa's face to paste on the front of each envelope.

She showed them how to cut out the coupons.

Soon the Pee Wees were busy.

Thinking.

Writing.

Then cutting and thinking and writing some more.

Roger decorated his coupons around the edge with a border.

"How about a coupon for bringing your mother and father breakfast in bed?" said Molly to Mrs. Peters.

"That is a very nice gift," said Mrs. Peters. "I would love to have a coupon for breakfast in bed on Christmas morning."

"I wish I had thought of that," said Lisa.

"Well, you didn't," said Molly.

"Can we make a breakfast-in-bed

10

coupon?" asked Kenny Baker. Kenny was Patty's twin brother.

"Of course," said Mrs. Peters.

Almost everyone made a coupon for breakfast in bed.

"Copycats!" said Molly. "That was my idea!"

"Mrs. Peters said it was okay," said Tim Noon. "We can all make them."

Soon the Pee Wees had lots and lots of colored coupons.

"I've got twenty-two!" shouted Roger.

"Make sure you can do all of your favors, Roger," warned Mrs. Peters.

"Yeah, Roger," said Tracy. "Show-off."

Molly put her coupons in the envelope. She had ten. They were good favors. Hard favors. She pasted Santa's face on the envelope. It was a wonderful present!

While the Pee Wees cleaned up the

room, Mrs. Peters went upstairs to make hot chocolate for everyone.

"When is Mrs. Peters's baby coming?" whispered Mary Beth to Molly.

"In December," said Molly.

"It is December!" said Mary Beth. "Maybe it will come today."

Molly began to laugh. "Babies don't come to Scout meetings," she said. "They come to hospitals."

"The stork brings babies," said Sonny.

"The stork!" repeated Tracy. "I've got lots of babies in my family and no stork ever brought any of them!"

"How can a bird bring a baby?" Molly laughed.

Molly wasn't exactly sure how babies came, but she knew a bird didn't bring them.

While the Pee Wees drank hot chocolate and ate Christmas cookies, Mrs. Peters talked about caroling in the shopping mall. "I'll bring songbooks," she said. "Mrs. Betz will come too. We'll be able to cheer up the shoppers with our Christmas songs."

"I love the mall!" said Lisa.

"Wear a tassel hat if you have one, and I'll bring some bells to shake. We'll all meet here next Friday afternoon," Mrs. Peters said. "It will be Christmas vacation, so we can get an early start. Now," she went on, "we will practice some songs, and then I'll teach you a new Pee Wee Scout Christmas song."

Mrs. Peters passed out booklets, and she gave each Scout a paper with the new song on it.

The Pee Wees sang some holiday songs they had learned in first grade.

"Frosty the Snowman."

"Rudolph the Red-Nosed Reindeer."

"Deck the Halls."

Then Mrs. Peters said, "We'll sing this new song to the tune of 'Jingle Bells.' Look at your papers."

14

Mrs. Peters sang the song through once. "Now you join me," she said.

The Scouts sang quietly at first. They sang the song over and over. When they knew the words they sang louder. Finally they could sing it without Mrs. Peters.

 Dashing through the snow,
Helping others out,
Laughing, playing too,
That's a Pee Wee Scout.

Bells on mittens ring,
Doing a good deed,
What fun it is to lend a hand
To someone else in need.

Pee Wee Scouts! Pee Wee Scouts!
We all come to say,
Oh, what fun it is to wish you
A happy holiday!

After that the Pee Wees joined hands and sang their regular Pee Wee Scout song. Then they said the Pee Wee Scout pledge.

Soon it was time to go home.

The Scout meeting was over.

But next week, Molly thought, we'll go caroling in the mall.

CHAPTER 2

At the Mall

Every morning Molly put a big X on her calendar. Each X was one day closer to caroling day. Soon every day in the week had an X on it. It was Friday at last.

The Pee Wee Scouts gathered at Mrs. Peters's house at two o'clock.

"It's a perfect day to go caroling," said their leader. "Snowy and cold."

The Scouts took off their coats and hats and mittens and boots.

Mrs. Peters passed out the songbooks.

She put her red tassel cap on and gave the Scouts some sleigh bells to shake. They jingled and jangled.

The Pee Wees practiced their carols and the new Pee Wee Scout Christmas song.

In a little while it was time to go to the mall. Mrs. Betz was already there.

The Pee Wee Scouts looked bright and cheery in their winter outfits. Sonny had a long red and green scarf around his neck. It was so long it almost reached his knees. His hat was red and green too. It had a pom-pom on top. "My mom knit it," he said proudly.

Sonny's mom could do everything, Molly thought. She skated better than the dads. She could paint and build things out of wood. And she could knit too.

At the mall, a man showed them where to stand. There was a little stage set up

for the Pee Wees. Right in the middle of the mall!

A big Christmas tree stood behind them.

On one side of the Scouts were tables where tired shoppers were drinking coffee and eating hot dogs.

On the other side was Santa Land and a big castle. Santa Claus was sitting inside!

Children waited in a long long line.

They waited to talk to Santa.

"Look!" shouted Sonny. "There's Santa Claus! We can tell him what we want for Christmas."

Roger snickered. Molly and Tracy laughed too.

Mrs. Peters and Mrs. Betz were showing the Pee Wees where to stand. The stage was made of three steps.

"Now, the shortest ones stand here in the front," said Mrs. Betz.

Patty and Sonny and Rachel stood on the first step.

"You aren't little," whispered Molly to Rachel.

"Yes I am," said Rachel. "My mom says I am tiny. And dainty."

But Rachel was much taller than Patty and Sonny. The other Scouts took their places along the steps. Roger went to the back. He was the biggest Pee Wee.

"Now, be careful and don't fall off the end," warned Mrs. Peters.

Roger gave Kenny a little shove. He didn't fall. But Mrs. Peters gave Roger a warning look.

Crowds began to gather in front of the Pee Wee Scouts. One little girl stared at Molly. She was eating popcorn and spilling most of it. Another little toddler with sticky hands was trying to grab Sonny's bright scarf.

Molly felt very grown-up. She remembered when her mother used to bring her to the mall to see the Christmas tree and hear the music. Now she was here singing. Just like a grown-up.

Mrs. Peters blew on her little pitch pipe. The Scouts began to hum. Mrs. Peters wanted them to all start on the same note. When she nodded, they all began to sing "Frosty the Snowman."

More shoppers stopped to watch and listen.

"This is fun," whispered Mary Beth. "I feel like we are movie stars."

When the Pee Wees finished "Frosty," the crowd clapped for them. Then they drifted away and a new group of shoppers circled around. One man began to sing with the Pee Wees when they sang "Silent Night."

A little boy came by with a beanshooter and shot beans at Tim.

"Hey, cut that out!" yelled Tim, in the middle of singing "The First Noel." "Mrs. Peters, he's shooting me!"

The little boy ran off.

All of a sudden, Molly's teacher, Mrs. Harris, came by.

"Look!" shouted Molly to the other Pee Wees who were in her class.

The Pee Wees waved.

Mrs. Harris waved back.

"You are very good!" Mrs. Harris called out.

The Scouts sang their Pee Wee "Jingle Bells" song. It was Molly's favorite.

"I want to sing 'We Three Kings,'" said Roger. "When can we sing that?"

"Next," said Mrs. Peters.

By three-thirty the Scouts were getting tired.

"I think we need a break," said Mrs. Peters. "Let's sit down and have some hot chocolate."

"That was hard work," said Mrs. Betz.

The Scouts scrambled off the steps and over to the tables nearby.

"Now," said Mrs. Peters. "Mrs. Betz and I are going into Ginger's store right here. We'll only be gone a little while. You all sit here and rest and don't leave this area. Do you understand?"

The Pee Wees nodded.

They were Scouts.

A Scout could be trusted.

But Sonny had his eye on the line leading to Santa's castle. His mother and Mrs. Peters were not even inside Ginger's when Sonny made a dash for Santa.

CHAPTER 3

Sonny in Santa Land

"**S**onny!" yelled Roger. "Hey, Sonny! Come back here."

But it was too late. Sonny was already standing at the end of the line. Molly could see him.

Sonny was the tallest one in Santa's line. His red and green hat popped up above the others. A little girl waited in front of him, eating a lollipop. She turned and pulled at Sonny's long scarf.

"I knew it!" said Molly. "Sonny still believes in Santa Claus!"

"I haven't believed in Santa Claus since I was a little kid," said Lisa. "When I was four."

"I haven't believed in him since I was two," said Kenny.

"I never believed in him," Roger said.

"You did too," said Tracy.

"That's dumb," said Roger. "How could he get down a skinny chimney? And he'd get full of dirt."

"He could," said Tim. "He's like Superman. He can do anything."

"You believe in Santa Claus too!" cried Molly.

"No I don't," Tim said.

"Ho, ho, ho!" Roger laughed. The other Pee Wees started laughing too.

At Tim.

And at Sonny.

Molly didn't laugh. It was not too long ago that she believed in Santa Claus. Last Christmas she believed. Just last year. Molly felt sad. She wished she still believed in Santa.

But not the stork! Or the tooth fairy. Poor Sonny, thought Molly. He's seven years old and he doesn't know yet.

The Pee Wees finished their hot chocolate and ran over to Santa Land to wait for Sonny.

"We're supposed to stay over there," said Mary Beth.

"Mrs. Peters said don't leave the area," said Lisa. "Santa Land is still the same area."

Molly didn't know how big an area was, but Mrs. Peters would be back soon. Mrs. Betz too.

Sonny was waving to them. He waved again.

"Get in line," he said. "You have to go to the end."

"We aren't going to talk to Santa," said Lisa, giggling.

Just then a two-year-old tried to push Sonny out of line and get ahead of him. But Sonny wouldn't move.

"That isn't Santa, anyway," said Lisa.

"It is too," said Sonny. "Who do you think it is, the Easter bunny?"

"It's a man dressed up in a red suit," said Roger. "With a pillow in his shirt." Roger patted his stomach.

"That's a lie," said Sonny. "It's really Santa."

The line was moving faster now. One little boy was crying too hard to talk to Santa. His mother had to take him away. Then another little girl had to go to the bathroom. So the line got shorter.

Sonny moved closer and closer to the front of the line.

"I've got a list in my pocket," said Sonny. "I put an X by the stuff I want the most. A robot and a spaceship set. And a build-your-own-dinosaur kit."

Roger was trying to drag Sonny out of line. "Come on, let's get out of here," he said.

But Sonny wouldn't budge. "You guys aren't going to get anything. Wait and see," said Sonny.

Molly just shook her head.

Soon the baby ahead of Sonny was sitting on Santa's knee. He pulled Santa's whiskers. Santa bounced him up and down on his knee. "Have you been a good boy?" Santa asked.

The photographer in front of the castle took a picture of the baby with Santa. Snap! Flash! The baby blinked.

Sonny was next.

The other Pee Wee Scouts leaned on

the wall of Santa's castle and watched. Sonny marched right up to Santa. He climbed up on his knee.

"Ouch!" said Santa. "My leg is breaking!" But Santa was joking. "How are you?" he asked Sonny. "Have you been good all year?"

"Look how big Sonny looks!" shouted Rachel. "He's too big for Santa's lap."

"I've been very good," Sonny was saying to Santa. Then he named all the toys he wanted. He handed Santa the list.

"This is so you don't forget," said Sonny.

"That's a big order," said Santa. "But I'll try to fill it."

Flash! went the camera. The photographer handed Sonny one picture.

Then Sonny slid off Santa's lap.

Santa patted Sonny on the head. Just like he patted the babies.

"Ho, ho!" Roger laughed. "Did he say he'd bring you a sackful of toys or a sackful of coal?"

"He said he'd try to bring me everything on my list. So there!" said Sonny.

"So there yourself!" roared Kevin.

By the time Mrs. Peters and Mrs. Betz came back, the Pee Wees were at the tables again.

"Did you have a good rest?" asked Mrs. Peters.

All the Scouts nodded.

"I talked to Santa Claus," said Sonny proudly. "He's going to bring me everything I want."

Mrs. Betz smiled. She said, "We'll put milk and cookies out for him and his reindeer on Christmas Eve."

"Let's sing a few more songs before we leave," said Mrs. Peters.

The Pee Wees scrambled back onto the steps with their sleigh bells.

"Let's sing 'Santa Claus Is Coming to Town!'" shouted Sonny. It was Sonny's favorite song.

Then they sang "We Wish You a Merry Christmas" and "The First Noel."

Last of all they sang their new Pee Wee Scout Christmas song. At the end of it they sang the chorus twice.

On the way home, Tracy said, "Someone should tell Sonny the truth. Everybody laughs at him. We don't want babies in the Pee Wee Scouts."

"Someone should tell him," agreed Molly. "But not me."

CHAPTER **4**

A Gift for Mrs. Peters

Molly had a lot of shopping to do. Christmas shopping. She wanted something special for Mrs. Peters. But what?

She had the Kindness Coupons for her mom and dad.

She got her grandma some flower seeds at the drugstore.

She bought her grandpa two of his favorite candy bars. With nuts.

She wanted to get Mary Beth a blue barrette to go with her new blue sweater.

But what could she get for Mrs. Peters?

When Mary Beth came over to play, Molly said, "What are you getting Mrs. Peters?"

"I don't know," she said. "I can't think of anything. Roger's giving her baseball cards."

"That's dumb," said Molly.

"He said she likes baseball. And she can chew the gum."

Roger's idea was no use to Molly.

Mrs. Peters would like something that was more personal. Something the Pee Wees made themselves.

Molly and Mary Beth sat down to think. Molly looked at the pictures hanging on her living room wall. Pictures of Molly when she was little. And of her relatives. Mrs. Peters would like pictures. Pictures of the Pee Wee Scouts.

36

"I know!" shouted Molly. "Let's make a Pee Wee Christmas tree!"

She ran and got a big sheet of green paper from her room. And her first-grade class picture. All the Pee Wee Scouts were smiling in the picture.

"The Pee Wees will be the ornaments!" she said.

Mary Beth looked doubtful. But she began to cut out the Scouts' faces.

Snip, snip, snip.

Nice and round.

Molly cut out a tree. A big green tree.

"Now!" she said. "We'll paste us on, for ornaments."

When all the pictures were on the tree, Mary Beth said, "It's beautiful!"

But Molly frowned. "It needs something else," she said. "Something more colorful. Like lights."

"We hang Christmas cookies on our tree," said Mary Beth.

"They are too big for this tree," said Molly.

Both girls saw the answer at the same time! There on the table in front of them was a dish of small mints. Tiny mints. In shiny bright paper. All different colors.

"That's it!" said Molly. She ran and got some Scotch tape. Then they taped the bright little mints all over the branches between the pictures. For lights.

"That's just what it needed," said Molly.

"Let's take it over to her right now!" said Mary Beth.

The girls got their coats on and started for Mrs. Peters's house. The tree was hard to carry. The wind blew it back and forth. Flap, flap, flap. It was big.

Just as they turned the corner of the block, they saw a black and white puppy coming toward them. When he saw the girls, his tail began to wag.

"I wonder whose dog that is," said Mary Beth.

"I never saw him before," said Molly. "He's wearing a blue collar."

Mary Beth patted his head and the puppy thought she wanted to play. He jumped up and licked her hand. "Down!" said Mary Beth. "Down, boy!"

Now the puppy was more excited. He began to bark. "Yip! Yip! Yip!"

He ran in circles around the girls. Molly held the tree over her head.

"He thinks you have something for him!" shouted Mary Beth.

The puppy leaped in the air. His tail was wagging.

"Run!" shouted Mary Beth.

But when Molly began to run, the puppy ran in front of her, barking and

jumping. The wind began to rip the branches on the Christmas tree.

"He smells those mints!" said Mary Beth. "He wants one!"

The puppy nipped at the tree branches. He tore at the pictures. The mints began to fall off. Some pictures of the Pee Wees fell off too.

The puppy's tail was wagging fast now.

"He's eating the paper and all," moaned Mary Beth. "He's going to eat the whole tree."

Sure enough, the puppy ate the mints. Then he ate two pictures. Then he ate a green branch of the tree.

The girls sat down on the curb. They felt like crying. The puppy was still tearing at the tree. There were only a few scraps of green paper left.

"Our present," cried Molly. Two tears rolled down her cheeks.

"All that work," said Mary Beth. She cried a little bit too.

The girls looked at the puppy. He had some green paper hanging out of his mouth. Then they looked at each other.

Suddenly Molly began to laugh.

Then Mary Beth laughed.

"Ho, ho," said Molly. "Merry Christmas, puppy!"

"He looks so funny," said Mary Beth.

"Bad dog!" cried Molly. She wanted to cry more, but all she could do was laugh.

"It wasn't his fault," said Mary Beth. "He thought the special present was for him."

CHAPTER **5**

Snowballs and Angels

The next day the girls went shopping. Mary Beth got Mrs. Peters two hankies with a *P* on each one. Molly got her a geranium plant that would have red flowers in the spring.

"They are wonderful!" Mrs. Peters said when the girls took the gifts to her house. She gave them both warm hugs. "These are very special gifts because they are from you," she said.

On the way home, soft snow began to

fall. It was getting dark early and Christmas lights twinkled in windows. A man on the street corner was ringing a bell. He was dressed like Santa.

"We should go caroling tonight," said Mary Beth. "It's a perfect night to carol."

"We could go to Mrs. Harris's house!" said Molly.

"And my grandma's," said Mary Beth.

"We need lots of us," said Molly. "It sounds better with lots of people singing."

When the girls got to Molly's, they told Mrs. Duff their plan. "I'll come too!" she said. "And I'll call Mrs. Noon and Mrs. Baker."

Before long there were lots of Pee Wees who wanted to come. And lots of moms and dads.

Mrs. Peters said she would come and bring the bells.

Tim brought his little brother. "He

can't sing, but he can ring bells," said Tim.

It must be fun to have a little brother, thought Molly. Especially at Christmas. Molly hated being an only child at Christmas. Rachel was an only child too. But she liked it. And Sonny was an only child. All the other Pee Wees had brothers and sisters.

The Pee Wees sang as they walked up and down the snowy streets. They stopped in front of houses that were lit up, and sang.

"Come in," said one man, who walked with a cane. "Come in and sing for me."

It was fun to go to different houses. The man said his name was Mr. Judd.

He showed them pictures of his family. His piano was filled with pictures. "I'm all alone now," he said. "And you came to cheer me up."

The Pee Wees sang "Frosty the Snowman."

And "Jingle Bells."

And their own Pee Wee Scout Christmas song.

Then Mr. Judd gave them each a candy bar.

"I'll bet they are from Halloween," whispered Kevin. "Left over."

"Come again," said Mr. Judd as the Pee Wees went away.

The snow was falling softly now as they walked and sang.

Rachel taught the Pee Wees a Hanukkah song. They sang that too.

My Dreidel

I have a little dreidel
I made it out of clay,
And when it's dry and ready,
Then dreidel I shall play.

O dreidel, dreidel, dreidel,
I made it out of clay,
O dreidel, dreidel, dreidel,
Now dreidel I shall play.

"That is very pretty," said Mrs. Peters. "We all learned something new tonight."

The Scouts sang at Mrs. Harris's house. "Merry Christmas!" she said. She gave them some hot chocolate.

They sang at Mary Beth's grandma's house. And at Tracy's uncle's.

Then the Pee Wees began chasing one another through the piles of snow. Roger scooped up a handful of snow and made a snowball. He threw it at Patty. Patty scooped up some snow and threw it back. They chased each other around the corner.

"Hey, Patty cake, baker's man, throw me a snowball as fast as you can!" shouted Roger. He dashed away from her.

Patty ran after him with a snowball. Soon all the girls were throwing snow at Roger.

"I think Roger likes Patty," whispered Lisa to Molly.

"All the Pee Wees like each other," said Molly. But she knew what Lisa meant. She meant that Patty was Roger's girlfriend.

"He likes her best," said Lisa.

Now Roger was washing Patty's face with snow.

Lisa is right, thought Molly. Roger does like her best. Patty is cute. And nice. No wonder Roger likes her.

Molly felt shy around Patty now. She wondered if any boy would ever like her that way. And think she was cute. And wash her face with snow.

"Boy, I'm tired," said Tim, falling down on purpose in a big snow pile.

"You made an angel!" said Tracy to Tim. "Look, you made an angel in the snow!"

All the Scouts lay down in the snow to make angels. They moved their arms up and down to make wings. Even some of the moms and dads made angels. Big mom and dad angels!

"It's a whole angel family!" shrieked Rachel. "Pee Wee angels and all their relatives!"

"I'm going to make horns on mine," said Roger. With his hands he made two horns on his angel.

"Not on mine you don't!" yelled Patty. But it was too late. Roger dashed over to Patty's angel and made horns on hers too.

"It's a devil now!" cried Patty.

Before long the Pee Wees were all rolling in the snow, and the angels disappeared.

As they started for home, they heard the tinkling of a bell. Not their own bells.

"Look!" shouted Sonny. "It's Santa! In front of the store!"

Dr. Meyers and Mrs. Ronning put some money in Santa's red kettle.

"Thank you, and Merry Christmas," said the Santa.

"Do you remember me?" asked Sonny. "I'm the one who gave you the long list in the mall."

Santa smiled at Sonny. He looked different to Sonny.

The Pee Wee Scouts burst into laughter.

Suddenly Molly felt bad, laughing at Sonny. She always laughed at him with the rest of the Scouts. It was no fun to be laughed at. She knew how bad it felt.

Molly believed in Santa just last year. She felt awful when people had laughed at her for it.

She wanted to protect Sonny. He had to find out the truth so that people wouldn't laugh at him.

"Someone has to tell Sonny the truth," said Molly to Mary Beth. "Everyone thinks he's a baby."

"Who?" said Mary Beth. "I don't want to tell him. He'll get mad."

"Then I'll have to," said Molly bravely. "But not right now."

Mad or not, Molly had to save Sonny. Or else he'd still believe in Santa when he was in high school! Then everyone would really laugh.

If no one else would tell him, Molly would just have to do it herself. She didn't want to. And she didn't know how. But she knew she had to stop Sonny from being such a baby. She had to save him!

CHAPTER 6

Scouts to the Rescue

On Christmas morning, Molly's grandma and grandpa came over early. The whole family opened their gifts together. Her grandma and grandpa liked their gifts. They gave Molly big hugs. Christmas hugs. And her mom and dad liked their coupons.

"Now!" said Mr. Duff. "I will have some help around here."

Molly laughed.

Her mom said, "I can't wait to have my breakfast in bed."

Molly got a music box from her parents. It played Brahms's lullaby when the cover was lifted.

She got a scarf and mittens from her grandma. "I knit them myself," her grandma said.

She also got a Barbie doll and clothes. And a miniature sewing machine to make her dolls some more clothes. And a new board game.

Christmas was fun! Everything was so shiny and new. The lights on the tree sparkled brightly. Smells of the Christmas dinner cooking filled the house.

"Why don't you ask Rachel over for Christmas dinner?" said Mrs. Duff to Molly. "Rachel's family doesn't celebrate Christmas. It would be fun to share the day with her."

Rachel was not Molly's best friend.

Sometimes she made Molly mad. But Molly liked her sometimes.

Molly ran to the phone.

"Really?" said Rachel. "I'll come right over!"

Rachel was at the door in no time. "It smells so good in here," she said. "We're just having sandwiches at our house."

Rachel rubbed her stomach.

Before dinner, Molly and Rachel played Molly's new board game. Rachel won twice and Molly won once.

It was fun to share Christmas with Rachel! It was like having a sister. There were no games you could play alone. And Rachel was a good player.

At dinner there were candles on the table. And lots of good food. Rachel had two helpings of dressing and gravy. And two pieces of pumpkin pie. Molly's grandpa told stories of his Christmases long ago.

After dinner the girls played some more. They colored and cut paper dolls. Molly's dad took pictures with his new camera. Then he took a Christmas nap.

Molly's grandpa and grandma dozed off on the sofa. But Molly and Rachel ate Christmas cookies and fruitcake and ribbon candy.

"I'm stuffed!" said Rachel. "You have a lot of food at Christmas."

When it began to get dark, Molly and her dad walked Rachel home.

"Thank you," Rachel said, giving Molly a shy little hug. "Next year you can come over on one of the Hanukkah nights."

"That would be fun," said Molly.

When they got back home, Molly's mom had a fire going in the fireplace. She turned on the tree lights again. Molly's grandpa read her some stories from a new book. It felt cozy and warm in the house when the street lights came on outside. It got dark early.

Christmas was all over. It had been a good one for Molly.

After Christmas, it began to snow harder than ever. Snow piled up in Molly's front yard. It made a drift in front of the door. Car wheels spun when they got going in the mornings.

Early one morning, the phone rang.

Molly answered it.

It was Mr. Peters!

"I wonder if the Pee Wees can give us some help," he said. "It is time to go to the hospital for the baby, and our driveway is full of snow! We may have trouble getting out. If all the Scouts helped, I think we could do it."

Mrs. Peters's baby was coming!

"I'll call everybody," said Molly. "We will come right over."

"Wonderful," said Mr. Peters. "Thank you."

How exciting! thought Molly.

Quickly, she called the other Pee Wees. Roger and Sonny were still in bed, but their mothers said they'd wake them up.

Molly got out her new scarf and mittens. She put on her coat and boots. Her mother helped her.

"This is a real Pee Wee emergency!" said Mrs. Duff.

Molly took the snow shovel and started walking through the big drifts of snow in front of her house.

When she got to the street, she met Sonny. His mom was with him!

"I couldn't get in to work today," she said to Molly. "So I thought I would come and help out." She and Sonny both carried snow shovels over their shoulders.

When they got to Mrs. Peters's house,

Tim and Kevin were already there. Roger came next. Before long, all the Pee Wee Scouts were helping.

Puff, puff, puff.

The shovels went into the soft fluffy snow.

Puff, puff, puff.

The Pee Wees breathed hard.

Shoveling was hard work.

The shovels hit the driveway.

Scrape, scrape, scrape.

"This snow is deep," groaned Rachel.

"Many hands make light work," called Mrs. Betz, who was always cheerful.

She was right. The drifts began to disappear.

Puff, puff, puff.

Scrape, scrape, scrape.

The Pee Wee Scouts sang songs as they shoveled. It was fun to do a real good deed. An emergency good deed. They

had to get Mrs. Peters to the hospital on time!

As they shoveled, Sonny said, "I think babies should come in the summer. When there is no snow."

Mr. Peters laughed. So did all the Pee Wees. But secretly, Molly thought it would be a good idea. She didn't think it was funny.

"Babies don't always come when you want them to," said Mr. Peters. "They usually come in bad weather or in the middle of the night."

"If you don't get there on time will they give the baby to someone else?" asked Sonny.

"No," said Mrs. Betz quickly. "The stork always brings the right baby to the right mother."

Now the Scouts really snickered. They did not know everything about babies, but they all knew that the stork did not bring them.

"I know where babies come from," Tracy whispered to Molly. "I know everything about babies."

Molly wanted to ask Tracy to tell her. But then Tracy would think she was a baby too. "I do too," Molly lied.

Soon the driveway was clear. "I'll be able to get the car out now," said Mr. Peters.

Mr. and Mrs. Peters got into the car. They thanked the Pee Wee Scouts over and over. Mrs. Peters threw kisses to them as they started for the hospital.

The Scouts stood in the driveway waving.

We did it! thought Molly. We did the best good deed yet. It made her feel good.

The Scouts stayed to play for a little while. They began to throw snowballs. And they told each other what they got for Christmas.

"I got everything on the list that I gave Santa," boasted Sonny. "Every single thing. I told you I would."

A few Scouts laughed.

"And I found a reindeer hoofprint in my backyard too," Sonny added.

"It's probably a dog's footprint," said Tracy.

"It's a reindeer's," said Sonny. "I looked it up in my nature book."

"Sonny, Sonny, baby Sonny!" sang Roger and Rachel together.

Molly didn't laugh. She felt sorry for Sonny. He didn't have a sister to tell him things. And Mrs. Betz was no help.

Molly had to help him. Or the whole

65

world would laugh at Sonny! But what should she say?

The stork.

Santa Claus.

She had to think of a way.

CHAPTER 7

The Snow Pee Wees

Mrs. Betz and the other parents took their shovels and started for home. But the Scouts still had lots of pep. The sun came out and the snow grew sticky. Snowman-sticky, thought Molly.

She began to push a snowball across the ground. It got bigger and bigger.

"Hey," she called. "Let's make a snowman for Mrs. Peters!"

"We can make eleven snowmen with all this snow we shoveled," said Kevin.

"Eleven Pee Wees!" said Tim. "We can make Mrs. Peters and all eleven of us!"

The Pee Wees got right to work, rolling big balls out of snow. As Molly's ball got bigger, it got heavier to push.

She worked and worked.

And shoved and tugged.

At last she got the ball of snow right in front of the Peterses' living room window.

Then she began to roll another. And another. She needed help to lift the head on top of the second ball.

"This has to be the head," said Roger. He and Kevin helped Molly push it up on top. "We can't get another ball on top of this."

"I'll carve arms in the sides," said Molly. When she finished the arms, she fixed the face and ears and hair.

"We should each make our own self,"

68

said Kevin. "Then we can all make Mrs. Peters."

"And the baby!" shouted Lisa.

Molly looked at her snow Pee Wee. It didn't look like her. Her hair was fluffier. She got more snow and added it to the top for hair.

"I've got an idea," she said. "I'll be right back."

Molly ran home quickly and got one of her old hats, and some mittens. And her Pee Wee kerchief.

She told her mother what they were doing.

Then Molly dashed back and put her red cap on the snowman's head. She tied her kerchief around the neck. She filled the mittens with snow and put them where the hands should be. And she put some big round buttons on the front.

"What are those for?" asked Lisa.

70

"Those are my badges," said Molly proudly.

Some of the other Scouts dashed home too. They came back with some Pee Wee kerchiefs and badges. The Scouts put them on the snowmen.

Except Tim's. His snowman was behind all the others. In the back.

"I want mine plain," he said. "Snowmen should be white."

"These aren't snowmen," said Patty, laughing. "They're snow Scouts."

"Look at Rachel's!" shouted Tracy.

Rachel's Pee Wee was wearing a dance tutu and toe shoes. She had even put a sparkly crown on the head made from an old necklace.

"Tracy's is fat!" shouted Kevin.

Tracy had stuffed the arms of her old jacket with snow. Her snowman did look fat. It looked round and funny.

"It doesn't look like you," said Lisa.

"They don't have to be perfect," said Tracy.

"My head keeps falling off!" cried Sonny.

"You have to pack the snow, dummy," said Roger.

But it wasn't the snow.

It was Kevin.

"Kevin is pushing it off when you aren't looking," Kenny told Sonny.

Sonny began to chase Kevin in and out among all the snow Pee Wees.

Poor Sonny, thought Molly. Everybody picks on him. She made a new head for Sonny's snowman.

Roger and Patty were rolling big balls of snow to make Mrs. Peters. They rolled them right into the middle of the group.

"Let's make a chair for her to sit on,"

said Tracy. "Because she has to hold the baby."

Tracy pushed up a big chunk of snow behind her.

"Ho! It looks like a beach ball!" Roger laughed.

"It's a chair," said Tracy crossly.

Kenny rolled a small ball of snow and put it in Mrs. Peters's arms.

"Wait!" called Tracy. She lifted the baby up and put an old scarf around it. "It's a blanket," she explained.

Molly stepped back to look at Mrs. Peters and all the snow Pee Wees.

Some were little.

Some were big.

They were all smiling.

Most of them had on badges and kerchiefs.

"Won't Mrs. Peters be surprised when

she comes home from the hospital," said Molly.

"The baby looks real," said Lisa softly. "It looks like Mrs. Peters is singing to it."

"I'm hungry," said Sonny. "I'm going home to eat."

All the Scouts were hungry. They had worked hard in the fresh air. It was time to go home.

Molly could hardly wait for Mrs. Peters to see their surprise.

CHAPTER 8

The Littlest Scout

That night Molly's phone rang. It was Mrs. Betz. "Good news!" she said. "Mrs. Peters had a baby boy!"

It was finally here. A brand new little baby. Molly secretly wished it was a girl. Then they could name it Holly to rhyme with Molly.

"I have to call everyone," said Mrs. Betz, hanging up.

The next morning Mr. Peters called. "There's a big family in my front yard!" he said.

Molly giggled. "Those are snow Pee Wees!" she said.

Mr. Peters wanted all the Scouts to come over so he could take their picture. When they got there, each Scout stood next to the snowman he or she had made.

"Smile!" called Mr. Peters. Click!

"Now we can show Mrs. Peters. Just in case they melt," he added.

Two days later, Mrs. Peters came home. The snow Pee Wees were still there. But they were very very small. They were melting.

"Snow doesn't last forever," said Molly's mother at supper that night.

Molly felt sad.

Christmas vacation went fast. Molly was glad when school started again. That meant Scout meetings would start again soon.

Monday was the day before the meeting. At recess Rachel said, "I'm bringing the baby a present. It's a little silver spoon to feed the baby with."

"A new baby can't eat with a spoon, dummy," said Roger. "They just drink milk."

"Dummy yourself," she said. "He will be eating cereal in a few weeks."

"How could he hold a spoon?" asked Sonny. "He can't chew cornflakes without teeth."

"You hold the spoon for babies." Rachel sighed. "You have to feed them mushy stuff. Like oatmeal."

"Yuck," said Sonny. "I hate oatmeal."

On Tuesday, most of the Scouts brought little presents for the baby. Molly brought a little yellow stretch suit. Her mother had wrapped it.

Rachel's present had a little rattle tied in the bow.

"Come in!" called Mrs. Peters.

She wasn't fat anymore, Molly noticed.

The Scouts filed in quietly. Mrs. Peters's house looked different today.

It smelled different too. It smelled like baby powder. There were boxes of diapers on the table. And packages and cards around.

But most important, there was a wooden cradle in the living room. And in the cradle was the new baby!

Troop 23 made a circle around the cradle so they could all see him at once.

"Rat's knees!" said Molly. "He's so small!"

She had never seen a baby so small.

"Look at his little nose!" cried Patty.

"Where's his hair?" asked Tim.

"He looks soft," said Lisa. "Soft and pink."

"Look at his tiny little fingers," said Rachel. "Oooochy, cooochy!"

"He is almost as pretty as Lucky," said Roger with a snicker. Lucky was a dog.

Molly wanted to hold the baby. And give him a hug.

The Pee Wee Scouts sat down in a circle and gave Mrs. Peters their packages.

"What a nice little suit!" she said. "He will wear it tomorrow when he goes to the doctor. Thank you, Molly.

"And he doesn't have a feeding spoon," said Mrs. Peters to Rachel. "It is just what he needs!"

Rachel made a face at Roger.

Sonny pushed a big box toward Mrs. Peters. It did not look like a gift. "My mom sent these," he said, "for the baby. They're my old baby clothes."

"Why, thank you, Sonny! These will come in handy," said Mrs. Peters.

She opened the carton and took out a little white cap and a stuffed dog. Then she held up a little sunsuit with a boat on it.

Sonny turned red.

A few Scouts laughed out loud.

"I'll look at the rest of these later," said Mrs. Peters, closing the box.

"What is the baby's name?" asked Mary Beth.

"His name is Nick," said Mrs. Peters. "After his grandpa. And because he was born around Christmas."

Molly liked the name Nick. If he could not be called Holly to rhyme with Molly, Nick was the next best thing.

"Yeah!" The Pee Wees cheered. Some of them whistled, to show they liked his name.

Then they got quiet. Nick was sound asleep.

"Now that he is sleeping," said Mrs.

Peters, "let's go into the kitchen for our meeting."

The Scouts followed her.

"The first thing we must do today is give out some badges," said Mrs. Peters.

Mrs. Peters held up a red badge. It showed a Scout holding a songbook. And wearing a tassel cap. The Scout's mouth was open, in the shape of a big O. "This is a badge for caroling in the mall," Mrs. Peters said.

"And this one," she went on, holding up a white badge, "is even more important! It is the Helping Out in an Emergency badge."

This badge had a big *E* on it, and a picture of a helping hand. It wasn't as pretty as the caroling badge, but Mrs. Peters said it was very important.

"This is the badge for shoveling the snow so we could get to the hospital," said Mrs. Peters. "Thank goodness for all of you!"

Everyone clapped and cheered.

As Mrs. Peters called out the names, the Scouts came up one by one. Mrs. Peters pinned their new badges on their blouses and shirts.

When they all had their badges, the Pee Wees cheered and clapped all over again. Molly felt proud.

Mrs. Peters put some cookies out on the table. And some hot chocolate.

"Before long," she said, "spring will be here. We will go for nature walks in the park. And plant gardens."

"We can help push the baby stroller," said Mary Beth.

Mrs. Peters laughed. "The baby will have so much attention he will be spoiled," she said. "When he cries during a Scout meeting, there will always be someone to hold him!"

But Nick did not cry at his first meeting. Molly hoped and hoped he would. She wished she could wake him up. But he slept right through the whole meeting.

When the Scouts finished their cookies, they joined hands and sang the Pee Wee Scout song. Then they said the Pee Wee Scout pledge.

They told Mrs. Peters about doing the favors on their Kindness Coupons.

"My mom hopes we make Kindness Coupons again next Christmas," said Lisa.

"My mom wants some for her birthday," said Kevin.

The Scouts cleaned up the kitchen and went into the living room to watch the baby.

"Look, he is smiling in his sleep!" said Mary Beth.

"That's gas," said Tracy. "He is too little to smile."

"I'm afraid she's right," said Mrs. Peters. "Nick is just two weeks old today."

The meeting was over. The Scouts were ready to go home. It's now or never, Molly thought. She had to tell Sonny about Santa Claus!

She tapped him on the shoulder as he was putting his jacket on.

"Sonny," she whispered bravely. "There isn't any real Santa Claus. Your mom gives you the things on your list. I used to believe in him too. But when you're seven you should know."

"I know that," said Sonny. "I knew he wasn't real. I saw his beard. It was just pasted on."

Rat's knees! Molly stamped her foot. "Then why did you say he was real?"

"I was just pretending," said Sonny,

zipping up his coat. "It's more fun to believe."

"But people laugh at you," Molly argued.

"Hey," called Sonny to the rest of the Pee Wees. "I don't believe in Santa Claus anymore. I was just pretending."

"About time," said Roger, putting on his mittens.

"Sonny is still a baby though," whispered Tracy to Molly. "He may not believe in Santa Claus, but he still believes in the stork."

Maybe he does, thought Molly. But he'll have to find out about babies by himself!

Mrs. Peters waved to the Pee Wee Scouts as they walked down the street toward home.

Pee Wee Scout Song

(to the tune of
"Old MacDonald Had a Farm")

Scouts are helpers, Scouts have fun
Pee Wee, Pee Wee Scouts!
We sing and play when work is done,
Pee Wee, Pee Wee Scouts!

With a good deed here,
And an errand there,
Here a hand, there a hand,
Everywhere a good hand.

Scouts are helpers, Scouts have fun,
Pee Wee, Pee Wee Scouts!

Pee Wee Scout Pledge

We love our country
And our home,
Our school and neighbors too.

As Pee Wee Scouts
We pledge our best
In everything we do.